THE Christmas HAT

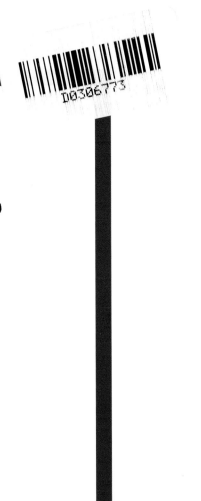

by A.J. Wood

illustrated by Maggie Kneen

PIPPBROOK
BOOKS

LITTLE OWL was just a tiny baby
when Rabbit and Badger found him
lost in the woods one fine autumn day.

"Don't worry, Little Owl," Rabbit had said kindly,
stroking his downy head. "We will take care
of you until you are big enough
to take care of yourself."

Rabbit and Badger loved Little Owl,
but looking after him could
sometimes be tricky....

"Don't do that,
Little Owl!"
said Rabbit.

"Or that!"
said Badger.

"And definitely not that!"
added their friend Mole as Little Owl
began unravelling his favourite blanket.

When winter came,
the animals could not even see
what mischief Little Owl was getting into.
His fluffy white feathers blended so
perfectly with the snow that he
seemed to disappear!

"Only a few days until Christmas," said Rabbit
happily one snowy morning. As she put the finishing
touches on her Christmas cake, she had an idea.

"I will make Little Owl a hat for Christmas,"
she said to Badger. "A bright red hat to wear when he
goes outside. That way we will always be able to see
where he is and what he is up to."

Little Owl liked his soft, red present,
but he wasn't quite sure what
to do with it at first.

"Wear it when you go out
in the snow," instructed Rabbit.
"Then we will always
be able to find you."

To Little Owl
love Santa
xxx

Later that day, the animals
went for a walk in the snowy wood.
As usual, Little Owl was
lagging behind, hopping in
and out of snowdrifts.

"Well, at least we can see
where he is now,"
Rabbit said to Badger.

But just then,
something terrible happened.

From behind the trees
sprang a big red fox, looking
for something tasty to eat for
his Christmas dinner.
The other animals ran
for cover, but Little Owl
just stopped hopping
and stayed very still.

He thought the snow would hide him,
as it usually did. But he had forgotten all
about the new red hat on his head.

The fox licked his lips. "Hello, Little Owl," he said.
"In that nice red hat you look good enough to eat!"
"Run, Little Owl!" cried the animals from their hiding place.
"Run away as fast as you can!"

So Little Owl ran, bouncing and tumbling
through the snow. The fox was hot on his tail until...

Whumphf!

Down a snowbank fell Little Owl,

and off came his bright red hat.
He sat down hard in the snow
and stayed very, very still.

Fox looked everywhere, but he couldn't see Little Owl.
He slunk off into the woods, his tummy
still rumbling with hunger.

"Thank goodness you're safe!" cried Badger.
Rabbit gave Little Owl an extra-cuddly hug as
they headed back home. "Maybe that nice red hat
wasn't such a good idea after all," she said.

But Little Owl loved his soft,
red hat. It didn't take him long to find
just the perfect use for it.

And Rabbit and Badger always knew
exactly where to find him at bedtime.

For Sass with love, Maggie
For Oscar, who looks good in a hat—A.J.W. (alias The Mother Bird)

PIPPBROOK BOOKS

First published in the UK in 2004 by Templar Publishing

This paperback edition published in 2015 by Pippbrook Books,

an imprint of The Templar Company Limited,

part of the Bonnier Publishing Group,

The Plaza, 535 King's Road, London, SW10 0SZ

www.templarco.co.uk

www.bonnierpublishing.com

Illustrations copyright © 2004 by Maggie Kneen
Text and design copyright © 2004 by The Templar Company Limited

3 5 7 9 10 8 6 4 2

978-1-78370-528-3

Designed by Janie Louise Hunt
Edited by Sue Harris

Printed in Malaysia 0280916